The Secret Cave
of Robinwood

The Secret Cave of Robinwood

Written by Paul McCusker

Illustrated by Karen Loccisano

PUBLISHING

Colorado Springs, Colorado

THE SECRET CAVE OF ROBINWOOD

Copyright © 1992 by Focus on the Family

Library of Congress Cataloging-in-Publication Data

McCusker, Paul, 1958-
  The secret cave of Robinwood / Paul McCusker ; illustrations by Karen
Loccisano.
    p.   cm. — (Adventures in Odyssey ; 3)
  Summary: To impress the members of a special boys'club he longs to join, Mark
betrays a secret of his best friend Patti, causing him to lose her friendship and his
club membership.
  ISBN 1-56179-102-4(pbk.) :
  [1. Friendship—Fiction. 2. Clubs—Fiction. 3. Conduct of life—Fiction.]
I. Loccisano, Karen, ill. II. Title. III. Series: McCusker, Paul, 1958-   Adventure
in Odyssey ; 3
PZ7.M47841635Se   1992
[Fic]—dc20   91-11
                                                                       CIP
                                                                       AC

Published by Focus on the Family Publishing, Colorado Springs, CO 80995.

Distributed in the U.S.A. and Canada by Word Books, Dallas, Texas.

Editors: Sheila Cragg and Janet Kobobel
Designer: Sherry Nicolai Russell
Cover and Interior Illustrations: Karen Loccisano

Adventures in Odyssey Radio Drama
(A Focus on the Family Production)
Creators: Phil Lollar, Steve Harris
Executive Producer: Chuck Bolte
Scriptwriters: Phil Lollar, Paul McCusker
Production Engineers: Dave Arnold, Bob Luttrell

Printed in the United States of America

92 93 94 95 96 / 10 9 8 7 6 5 4 3 2

*To Bob Adams, who shaped my
understanding of friendship.*

The Adventures in Odyssey novels take place in a time period prior to the beginning of the audio or video series. That is why some of the characters from those episodes don't appear in those stories — they don't exist yet.

Contents

1. Patti's Secret 1

2. The Green Curtain 9

3. An Invitation.. 17

4. Conflict of Interest 27

5. A Bang-Up Job 35

6. Betrayed 43

7. Double Deception 55

8. Exiled 63

9. The Search 71

10. The Scene Played Out 79

11. A Pleasant Surprise 89

CHAPTER ONE

Patti's Secret

S plash!

Mark Prescott let out a yelp, withdrew his spear from the cool mountain water and stood poised to make another thrust at his prey. For today, he wasn't Mark at all. He was Robin Hood dressed in woolen green hose that were soaked up to his leather britches. His matching, open-necked tunic was damp from all the splashing. Robin was fishing for dinner in LeMonde's River.

"I'm growing terribly hungry, sweet Robin," said Patti Eldridge, who wasn't Patti at all. She was Maid Marian resting on the river bank and watching Robin with an amusement she could barely contain. He had been trying to catch a fish for the better part of an hour.

"Do you doubt me, gentle one?" Robin asked.

Marian smiled as she tilted her face toward the afternoon sun and stretched out her legs, buried beneath several layers of her ruffled dress. "Never, but are you sure this is the best way to catch fish?"

Robin turned to her and said, "Have I spent the entire summer surviving in the forest with the men of Sherwood without knowing how to fish properly?"

"Dear, dear Robin," Marian sighed pleasantly.

"I suppose you know a better way," Robin said as he lunged forward with his spear.

"Blast!" he yelled, holding up his empty spear.

Marian giggled.

"It is for your sake that I soak myself to the bone, my lady," Robin said as his eyes carefully scanned the water. "Couldn't you bring me words of encouragement while I seek supper?"

"Breakfast, you mean," she jibed. "Why not let me try?"

"What? A fair and gentle woman?" Robin protested. "I cannot permit you to fish like a common gamekeeper."

"But I know the ways of the forest as well. Why can't you allow me to use what I know?"

"You can when you need to, my heart. But I am here, and I will do it. Ah!" he cried as he flung himself forward.

It was a faulty move. He overextended his reach, fell off balance, and with an enormous splash, spun headlong into the river.

Marian laughed loudly and fell helplessly back into the grass. "Maybe we should have gone out for hamburgers."

Robin sat in the water and blinked twice. With a dunking like that, he couldn't sustain his imaginary game any longer. He instantly returned to being Mark Prescott, a dark-haired kid in pullover, jeans and sneakers.

"Good grief," he sputtered.

Patti Eldridge—no longer a fair maiden in ruffles but a freckle-faced, blue-eyed young lady in baseball cap, shorts and T-shirt—rushed to the edge of the water.

"My hero!" she said, giggling.

Mark frowned. "It's not funny. I'll bet the real Robin Hood had his off days."

Patti held out her hand. "I think Robin Hood would have found a better way to catch fish."

"If you know so much about fishing, why don't you come in and catch a few?"

Mark reached for Patti's hand, grabbed hold of her wrist and pulled.

"Hey!" she screamed as she tumbled into the water.

"Oops," he said with a snicker.

"No fair." Patti wiped her face and splashed Mark.

He laughed and splashed her back, inciting a water battle. They finally called it quits when they began to cough from laughing so hard. Mark pushed away from her, half crawling, half swimming to the grassy bank. He climbed out and rolled onto his back.

"What about our fish?" Patti called.

"If you're so good, you catch them," he challenged, propping himself on his elbows to see what she would do.

"Okay," she said.

"You're crazy. You don't even have a spear."

"I don't need one." Her eyes moved quickly around the water. She froze in one position and said, "There's one."

He couldn't imagine what she thought she could do. Was she going to try and catch it with her hand? Mark sat up to watch.

In one swift motion, Patti snatched off her baseball cap, circled her arm through the air, scooped the cap into the water like a net and brought it out again. It was all done so gracefully Mark thought he could have been watching a ballet dancer.

"Tah-dah!" Patti smiled proudly. A small fish flapped about in her cap.

Mark instantly felt hurt because he had been shown up by a girl. But this wasn't just any girl, and he didn't want to spoil such a good day by getting mad. Besides it was a wonderful trick, so he applauded.

Patti bowed grandly once and then again. The third time, she swung her cap back into the water, allowing the squirming fish to escape.

Mark stood. "Let's go to Whit's End and get something real to eat."

Patti sloshed her way to the river's edge. "Okay. Maybe we'll be dry by the time we get there."

Mark held his hand out to her. She gripped it firmly, and he pulled her to the bank.

"Thanks," she said, smiling.

This time, without the mischief, the touch of their hands gave Mark a peculiar sensation. He suddenly realized that there was a time when he wouldn't have enjoyed such a simple afternoon of fun. Patti was a girl, after all. And girls shouldn't be good friends with boys—should they?

The answer to that question had been very slow in coming for Mark. But now, on this perfect August day as her hand slid from his, he knew they could. He didn't even care if some of the kids called them "boyfriend and girlfriend." Odyssey was a small town, and the others could have small thoughts if they wanted, Mark reasoned. Patti was as good a friend as any boy Mark had known.

All these thoughts flashed through Mark's mind in the few seconds his hand touched hers. He looked at Patti's eyes, half expecting them to show that she felt something similar. But her eyes were their usual blue and gave no hint that she had experienced the same feelings.

"I want you to tell me more about Robin Hood and his gang," Patti said. "I only saw the movie version."

As they strolled under a rich green canopy, Mark told her everything he knew about Robin Hood and the men of

Sherwood Forest.

Patti idly kicked at a broken branch in their path. "They had hiding places in the woods?" she asked with more than a casual amount of interest.

"Yeah," Mark answered, noting her tone. "Why?"

"No reason. Have you ever had a hiding place?"

"I built a tree fort with Tommy Smith when I lived in Washington, D.C.," Mark said. "What about you?"

"My bedroom at home has kind of been my hiding place. That's where I used to go to get away from everyone. But . . . it isn't the same as when I was little. I was going to fix it up before school started. My parents did it that sissy-looking pink."

"Pink's the right color for a girl," observed Mark.

"Not this girl! I want my room to be green like these woods. This is where I like to run. It's where I like to hide. My parents keep saying we'll repaint my room one of these days, but they put me off when I say I want to do it myself." She paused, glancing at Mark out of the corner of her eye. "I came up with a better place anyway."

"A better place?"

Patti's eyes widened with excitement. "Yeah! One in the woods, just like Robin Hood. In fact, that's what I named it, Robinwood. Neat, huh? But I haven't told anybody about it."

"Where is it? Can you show me?"

"Maybe," Patti said, suddenly playing it cool. "But you

have to promise not to tell anyone. Ever! Do you promise?"

"Sure," Mark said.

"Then follow me."

CHAPTER TWO

The Green Curtain

P atti led Mark to where the river fed into Trickle Lake. The warm sun had begun to dry their clothes by the time they had started up the mountainside. After they had hiked awhile, Patti suggested they stop on the pathway to take in the view of lush pines and sparkling water below.

The lake glinted like an open bag of diamonds. Mark had never seen the lake at this angle before. This trail was uncharted territory for Mark, like many parts of Odyssey.

It's beautiful, he thought. When he turned to say this to Patti, she had disappeared. Surprised, Mark spun around.

"Patti?" he called out.

How did she vanish like that? he wondered. *Is she hid-*

ing behind one of the trees? Maybe she hiked up the steeper side of the grade.

"Patti!" he yelled again.

She giggled.

Mark turned to see where the sound was coming from. Her voice seemed to be everywhere at once, but he still couldn't see Patti anywhere.

Patti laughed and said, "I'll bet Robin Hood didn't have a hiding place *this* good."

Again Mark turned around, now feeling foolish because he knew he must look foolish. He could feel his cheeks turning crimson.

"All right," he said. "Where are you?"

"Over here," she called.

Mark heard a rustling of branches.

Then, as if appearing out of thin air, Patti emerged from her hiding place. The illusion surprised Mark so much he blinked a few times to make sure he was seeing correctly. One moment he saw a wall of green foliage, the next moment Patti appeared in front of it.

"Neat, huh?" Patti said proudly, bowing like a magician.

Mark looked harder to see where Patti had disappeared. The scattered light, dense forest, heavy brush and ivy had played a trick on his eyes. On closer inspection, he could see that a lush green curtain was camouflaging the hillside.

Mark stared in wonder. A casual passerby would never have seen it. "What is it?" he asked.

"Come on," Patti said, spreading the green curtain aside and stepping into the darkness. "This is my hiding place."

She struck a match and lit a small candle stuck in the top of a soda bottle.

"I'll get a lantern later on," she added.

When Mark's eyes adjusted to the light, he could see that they were in a cave the size of a small room, with plenty of space to walk around. Patti had placed a table and a couple of wooden crates in the center to use as seats. Otherwise the cave was barren rock and dirt. Toward the rear, it continued on in darkness.

"What's back there?" Mark asked.

"I don't know. I didn't want to go back there alone."

Mark was going to tease her for being a chicken, but he thought better of it. He wouldn't want to go back into the yawning blackness by himself, either.

"Patti, this is a terrific hideout!" he exclaimed. "How did you find it?"

"Last weekend when your dad was visiting I got bored playing by myself and decided to look around the lake. While I was up here, I started to think about pirates. You know, like the ones you told me about in . . . in . . ." She furrowed her brow, trying to remember the name of the book.

"*Treasure Island?*" Mark offered.

"Yeah, that one. Anyway, I got to thinking about how they hid things in caves and wondered if maybe there was a cave around here somewhere."

"Pirates hid their treasures in caves near the sea, Patti," Mark said, correcting her. "This is just a lake."

"I know. I was just pretending," she answered defensively. "I kept thinking, where would I hide my treasure if I were a pirate? When I saw the bushes and ivy, I thought it would be neat if a cave was behind them. And it was!"

Mark was amazed as he looked around the cave. Maybe it had been here for thousands of years, and they were the first humans to set foot in it. Or maybe early settlers used it as a shelter. Or maybe it was the hideout for a notorious gang. Or maybe . . .

"I'm going to fix it up," Patti announced, interrupting Mark's flight of imagination. "I'm going to bring my own treasures up here."

"What kind of treasures?"

"My special private stuff. You know, my keepsakes and dolls and diaries."

Mark shivered. How could she use such a terrific hiding place to store dolls? It seemed like a waste to him. *This cave should be the scene of great adventures,* he thought. *A place to meet, to escape, to share secrets.*

"I think you could do better things than that with this cave," Mark suggested.

Patti frowned and shook her finger at him. "Oh, no you don't. This is my secret hideout. I'll share it with you, but you can't take it over."

Mark spread out his arms and shrugged innocently.

Patti put her hands on her hips. "I mean it, Mark Prescott!"

"I know, I know," Mark said.

Later, when Mark and Patti hiked back to Odyssey through the woods, they walked in silence. His mind buzzed with ideas for Patti's hideout. Oh, the things he could do with it. He imagined drilling a hole through the roof and installing a periscope, so they could see Trickle Lake. They could hang hammocks to sleep in and a table to eat on and real chests to store their treasures in and lanterns to see with. And maybe they could rig up a portable heater to use in the wintertime.

Mark shared some of his ideas with Patti. She seemed excited, too. She even helped him scheme how they might save money to buy such things.

In the midst of their brainstorming, Mark heard some loud talking in a section of the woods not far from their path. Mark slowed his pace and signaled Patti to be quiet.

"What's wrong?" she whispered.

"Don't you hear the kids talking?" Mark asked.

"So?"

"I think something's going on. Let's go see," Mark said. He made his way as quietly as he could through the fallen leaves; Patti followed a few steps behind. They reached the edge of a clearing and hid behind a tree. Only a few yards away a dozen boys were sitting in a small circle. It looked like they were having an Indian powwow.

"It's only the Israelites," Patti said, her voice full of disappointment.

Mark felt just the opposite. He had heard things about the Israelites and even had a brief encounter with them at the beginning of summer, shortly after he had moved to Odyssey. They were a gang of boys that often hung around Whit's End, the popular soda shop and discovery emporium run by John Avery Whittaker. It was rumored that they did different kinds of errands for Mr. Whittaker. Some of the kids in town claimed the Israelites performed good deeds for people in need.

Mark asked Mr. Whittaker about them once, but Whit dismissed them as a bunch of kids simply playing Old Testament characters. They dressed in leather vests and carried shields, spears, and bows and arrows. Mr. Whittaker thought it was healthier than pretending to be aliens from another planet or tortured heroes from the comic books.

The gang members had names like Jonathan, Ezer, Obadiah and Attai. Those weren't their real names, of course, but it allowed the kids to pretend while learning about the Bible. At least, that's how Mr. Whittaker had explained it.

As Mark watched the Israelites talk, he knew something more was going on, and he wanted to know what it was.

"I don't know why you're so interested in these guys," Patti whispered. She sat in the leaves and leaned against the tree.

"Just listen," Mark said, trying to hear what the Israelites were discussing.

He couldn't make out entire sentences. The tone of their voices was sharp, on edge. Whatever they were talking about, it sounded like they were having a serious disagreement.

He desperately wanted to hear the inner workings of this secret gang. Maybe he could find out who they really were and what they were up to. He crouched beside the tree, preparing to creep forward.

He glanced at Patti and started to gesture for her to stay still, but her expression quickly changed his mind. Her gaze was fixed on something behind him. Before he could turn around, a hand suddenly grabbed Mark's shoulder.

CHAPTER THREE

An Invitation

W hy were you spying on us?" demanded the leader of the Israelites.

Mark and Patti had been moved to the center of the clearing and were now surrounded by the gang.

Mark wanted to play it cool. He shrugged and said, "Just curious."

"You guys are always so overdramatic," Patti said scornfully. "Why would anybody want to spy on you? It's not like you have anything interesting to say."

"Don't be so rude, Patti," Mark said with a frown.

Patti glared at Mark, folded her arms and gnawed at her lip.

Mark looked back at the leader, who was called Jonathan, and said, "I've been interested in you guys ever since that time you took me to Whit's End. Remember?"

Jonathan nodded, so Mark continued, "I've heard a lot of good things about you."

"We've been hearing about you, too," Jonathan replied. He swatted at a fly buzzing around his curly, chestnut-colored hair. "All the kids know how you and Patti put Joe Devlin in his place and solved the mystery of the flat tire. We were impressed with that, weren't we?"

The other Israelites muttered their agreement, except one of them.

A boy with brown hair and a round, pudgy face grimaced. "I wasn't that impressed," he said.

Jonathan turned to him and replied, "Nothing impresses you, Attai."

"So?" Attai looked at Mark with half-closed eyes as if he were bored.

Jonathan returned his attention to Mark and Patti. "We were so impressed with your attitudes that we were thinking of asking you to join our gang. You would be our first girl member, Patti."

"You want us to join the Israelites?" Mark asked with surprise.

"I'm asking you to consider it," Jonathan answered. "There's a process for actually becoming a member."

Mark couldn't hide his enthusiasm. "Yeah! We'll do it!"

"No," Patti said simply.

Everyone turned and stared at her.

Is she crazy? Mark wondered. *They don't ask just anybody to be in the gang. This is an honor.*

"Patti!" Mark cried out. "What's the matter with you?"

Patti stood. "Look, I don't want to talk about this, and I don't want to hang around here anymore. Are you coming with me or not?"

Mark couldn't believe she was acting this way. "Patti, wait a minute. Think about it. Why don't you want to join the Israelites?"

"Why should I?" Patti countered. "It's just a silly gang. Why do we need to join a silly gang?"

"Because . . . ," Mark searched for an answer but couldn't find one. "Because!" he insisted.

Patti thrust her jaw out defiantly. "I'm not interested. It's a dumb idea."

She whirled on her heels and broke out of the circle of Israelites, walking away from them without looking back.

Mark jumped to his feet. "Can you wait?" he asked Jonathan as he started away. "I mean, can we still consider it? I'll . . . let me talk to Patti, and I'll tell you later." And then he stumbled over a small log, gathered himself up and ran to catch up with Patti.

"What's wrong with you?" Mark demanded when he reached her.

"There's nothing wrong with me," Patti replied. "I just

don't want to join their stupid gang, that's all."

"But, why not?"

"Because I don't want to. That's why."

"I don't get it," Mark said with a growl.

Patti halted in her tracks. "Why do you want to join them? What will the Israelites give you that we don't already have? It's been a great summer. We're having fun, so why do we need them?"

Patti didn't wait for an answer; she continued to walk.

After a second or two, Mark called after her, "Because they're a special kind of gang. Haven't you heard?"

"Hah!" Patti shouted over her shoulder.

Mark jogged to catch up to her. He was beginning to get angry. "Look, Patti. What will it hurt? Let's join and see what adventures we can have like Robin Hood and . . . and the three Musketeers."

Patti maintained her quick stride. "We've been having plenty of adventures without the Israelites, Mark. Just the two of us. Why do we have to have a gang?"

"We don't have to have a gang. Why do you keep asking me questions like that? I just think it would be lots of fun. It would be neat to be part of a gang like that."

Patti paused momentarily and scowled. "Then I feel sorry for you. I think it's good enough for the two of us to be friends and have fun. And I don't know why you have to spoil everything."

She started to move quickly down the path again.

"Where are you going?" asked Mark.

"Home!"

"But . . . but can't we talk about this?" implored Mark.

"No!" she replied curtly.

Mark frowned as he watched her hurry away.

"Girls!" he groaned to no one in particular.

Mark walked on alone to Whit's End. John Avery Whittaker, Whit as he preferred to be called, was behind the counter. He was experimenting with what appeared to be an ice-cream dispenser. His white hair seemed to accent the bobbing of his head as he peered into the machine, looked into another section and then checked the top of it again.

They exchanged hellos, and then Whit said, "If it doesn't work this time, I may have to scrap it and start over again."

"How does it work?" Mark asked.

Whit gestured with a screwdriver toward various mechanisms. "These scoops are supposed to dip the ice cream out of the containers and transfer it to the bowl over there."

Whit pointed to a small platform with a glass bowl on it. He turned back to the machinery and continued to calibrate and adjust different parts.

"But why do you need this? Are you getting tired of scooping the ice cream yourself?"

"My word, no!" A small spot of grease marred Whit's

thick white moustache.

"Then why?" Mark asked, giving Whit an inquisitive look.

"For the fun of inventing something. Good grief, Mark, inventions don't have to make life easier or do jobs I don't want to do. Sometimes they don't even have to work."

"Why bother?" Mark asked.

Whit smiled. "I find inventions to be worthwhile just for the experience of inventing them. Haven't you ever done something just for the experience of it?"

Mark thought about it for a moment. "Yeah, in fact, just today Patti and I got into a fight because I wanted to do something for the fun of it, and she didn't."

"And what was it that you wanted to do and Patti didn't?" Whit asked, tapping the screwdriver against something metallic on the inside of the ice-cream dispenser.

Strangely enough, Mark had a feeling Whit knew the answer to his own question. Whit was like that.

"Join the Israelites," Mark said.

"Oh? And why doesn't Patti want to join?" Whit asked, continuing to tinker.

"I don't know," Mark said. "She kept saying she thought it was dumb, and we don't need to join because we're having a lot of fun by ourselves and . . . and . . . that kind of thing. I can't figure her out sometimes."

Whit peered over the machine at Mark. "Really," he

said. "Do you think she's afraid the Israelites will wreck your friendship?"

The question surprised Mark. "What? Wreck our friendship? Why would she think that?"

"Oh, because it took you a long time to be her friend, and now that you are, she might be afraid of losing you," Whit said, disappearing behind the machine again.

"It's not going to wreck any friendship," Mark muttered.

Whit fastened a remaining bolt and then moved to the front of the ice-cream dispenser. "If you're sure of that," he said, "you might want to tell Patti."

That's the problem with having girls as friends, Mark thought. *You have to explain everything to them. Boys don't care. Boys just do things together. But girls always have to be assured.*

"Let's see if this thing works," Whit announced, rubbing his hands together. He flipped a switch on the side of the machine. The dispenser hummed. Then a mechanical arm reached over to the small container of ice cream, dipped into it like a bird going after bread crumbs and reappeared with a scoop of vanilla.

"So far so good," Whit said proudly.

The mechanical arm moved upward and then turned toward the glass bowl. Suddenly the machine popped and whined. The arm lurched backward and then sprung forward, propelling the scoop of ice cream at the glass bowl.

It was a direct hit. The bowl shattered on the floor.

Whit sighed, "Back to the old drawing board."

"Maybe you could use it for a catapult. The kids would like it for target practice," Mark offered.

Whit considered the suggestion. "You may have a good idea, Mark."

A few minutes later, while Whit was cleaning up the mess, he handed Mark a small note. Whit's eyes sparkled as if he were thinking of a joke he wanted to tell someone.

"I was asked to give this to you," Whit said.

Mark unfolded the note. On a plain piece of paper, these words were scribbled in blue ink:

If you still want to join ... The
gazebo in McAlister Park. Nine tonight.

CHAPTER FOUR

Conflict of Interest

Back home Mark walked into the kitchen just as Julie Prescott slammed down the receiver. His mother slumped into one of the dinette chairs and put her hands over her face.

"Mom?" Mark asked cautiously.

"He makes me so mad, I could . . . ," she said with a low growl.

Mark's heart sank; he knew she had been talking to his dad. When his parents had separated earlier that year, Mark was sure they would get a divorce. But over the past month, his parents had decided to try and work out their differences. They wanted to save their marriage, they had assured Mark. They wanted to be a family again. Mark had been living on the edge of that hope.

It was taking longer than Mark had thought it would. His parents squeezed in counseling sessions with the pastor when his dad could visit. They spent hours on the phone, sometimes talking softly, other times arguing like they were now.

What makes adults so weird? Mark wondered.

"You're not going to cry, are you?" he asked awkwardly.

"No," his mother said, her cheeks flushed with anger.

"Were you fighting again?"

She eyed her son curiously. "No, Mark, not really. Sometimes your father doesn't realize what he's saying. He has his own way of looking at things and can be very stubborn. It makes me mad."

"Are you still trying to get back together?" asked Mark anxiously.

"Yes, honey," she said, reaching out and pulling Mark close. "Don't let our little spats worry you. We're still trying to sort out our differences. We have to resolve certain things before we can live together again."

"But what's the problem?" he asked. "Why can't you guys just kiss and make up?"

His mother smiled sadly. "I wish it were that easy. You see, your father and I hurt each other. We said things we didn't mean. Our marriage didn't fall apart in one night— no marriage ever does. It was a slow breakdown, and the healing process is slow, too. It takes time to restore trust, and it takes work to rebuild love. Do you understand?"

"I'm trying to," he replied.

They were both quiet for a moment. Then his mother asked brightly, "So, what have you been doing today?"

Glad for the change of subject, Mark told his mother all about playing in the woods with Patti—leaving out the secret cave because he promised he would—and about meeting the Israelites and being asked to join their gang.

"A gang?" questioned his mother warily.

"A *good* gang, Mom. Nobody knows for sure, but we think Mr. Whittaker has something to do with it. The Israelites sometimes run errands for him."

His mother tapped the table thoughtfully. "Well, if Whit is involved, I'm sure it's all right."

"He gave me this note from them." Mark took the crumpled piece of paper out of his back pocket and handed it to her.

"Nine o'clock is awfully late to meet with a bunch of kids," she observed.

"It's not so late in the summer, Mom. The sun's barely gone down by then. Please, let me go. Please?"

She handed the note back to Mark and said, "I'm going to call Whit about this gang. I want to know what they're up to."

The conversation with Whit didn't last long; it consisted mostly of his mother saying, "Hmm" and "I see."

She asked a question or two and then hung up. Mark's curiosity was chewing him up, but he didn't want to nag his mother with too many questions. All he knew was she had agreed to let him meet with the Israelites at nine o'clock that night, and that was good enough for him.

For the rest of the afternoon, Mark prowled around the house nervously. He couldn't concentrate on anything or keep interested in the activities he usually enjoyed.

His mother finally suggested, "If you're so bored, you could clean your room."

"I'm not that kind of bored," he explained.

Finally he settled on the idea of writing a letter to his father. He sat at his desk, pushed away the clutter and started writing quickly. He put in the usual how-are-you-I-am-fine beginning; then he told his dad about the Israelites.

As Mark wrote, it dawned on him that he had discovered the answer to Patti's earlier question about why he wanted to be an Israelite. Becoming a member of the gang would give him a sense of belonging in Odyssey, and he wouldn't feel like an outsider anymore.

"Mark," his mother called from downstairs, "Patti's here."

Mark glanced at his watch. It was seven o'clock, just two hours before meeting the gang. He called back to have Patti come upstairs.

Patti entered silently, paced around the room, casually

picked up one of Mark's model cars and then flipped through the pages of a book.

"What are you doing?" she asked with strained casualness.

"Writing to my dad."

"What about?"

"Stuff," he said offhandedly. "What are you doing?"

Patti sat on the edge of Mark's bed. "I was thinking about going to the movies. You want to go?"

"I . . . I can't," he said.

"You're doing something with your mom?"

"No."

Patti's eyes narrowed. "Then why can't you go?"

Mark shifted from foot to foot uncomfortably and glanced away from her gaze. "I just can't, all right?"

"You're going to join the Israelites," she said flatly.

Mark didn't respond.

"You are," Patti continued. "I got one of those notes, too. They jammed it in my mailbox."

Mark looked at her hopefully. "Are you going?"

"No," she snapped. "We don't need to join a gang. They'll ruin everything."

"Why do you keep saying that? What will they ruin?"

"Us," she said.

Mr. Whittaker was right, Mark thought. *Mr. Whittaker is always right when it comes to these things.*

"No they won't," Mark insisted.

"Yes they will. You'll get all wrapped up with them, and we won't do things together anymore." Patti's tone was despondent.

"That's not true. If you join, we'll do things together all the time."

"With them," she said.

"So?"

"So, I don't want to run around with a gang. We're having fun by ourselves. I thought we were friends."

Mark bit his lip. Why did they even have to have this conversation?

"We are friends, Patti. Why does everything have to be such a big deal with you?"

"It's not a big deal!" shouted Patti. "If we're friends, then let's go to the movies tonight."

Mark didn't know what to do. Slowly he moved to his window and looked out onto the stretch of green grass below. A cat crept along the fence, its eye on something Mark couldn't see.

His back to her, he said, "I can't. I want to meet with the Israelites."

Mark's bed gave a gentle squeak as Patti stood. She stomped across the room and slammed the door as she left.

CHAPTER FIVE

A Bang-Up Job

Why did he have to make a choice? Mark wondered as he sat on the gazebo steps in McAlister Park. What was so wrong with wanting new friends? Couldn't he be friends with Patti and be an Israelite, too? She wasn't being fair.

Mark was so lost in his thoughts that he didn't hear the Israelites until they were almost behind him. Mark stood and looked expectantly at the group. They were all dressed in dark-colored clothes. Three of them were carrying bulging burlap sacks, but Mark couldn't tell what was in them.

"I told you he wouldn't be dressed right," complained Attai.

Mark glanced self-consciously at his white T-shirt.

"I didn't tell him," Jonathan said. "It's all right."

Then he turned to Mark and asked, "Are you sure you want to do this?"

"Uh-huh," Mark replied.

"Let's go." Jonathan waved for everyone to follow.

They moved with such purpose that Mark felt intimidated. He was the outsider here, as usual. He followed Jonathan closely, wondering if it would be dumb to ask where they were going.

They walked along silently. As they neared Fulton Street, Jonathan held up his hand. Mark heard a low rumble; then he saw headlight beams. The car went by without any hint that the driver had seen them.

"Okay," Jonathan said. "Obadiah, check it out."

The one called Obadiah ran across the street, looked around and then gestured for them to follow. They moved quickly. Mark imagined how it would look to a passerby to see a gang of boys wearing dark clothes.

"Where are we going?" whispered Mark, finally mustering the courage to ask.

"Quiet. We're not supposed to talk," Attai hissed.

Mark felt rebuked and lowered his head.

The Israelites followed LeMonde Street for a few blocks; then they turned onto Chatham Boulevard. Numerous trees and no street lights made it dark enough for them to move along without being noticed. The sounds of crickets and an occasional barking dog filled the night. Lights winked at them from the windows in warm, bright yellows and pale-blue television flashes.

Mark pictured the families behind those windows going about their usual summer night's business, totally unaware that a gang of boys was slipping past on a secret mission.

A wave of nervousness rolled through Mark. What were they doing, anyhow? What if they were doing something they shouldn't? Mark tried to calm himself by remembering that Whit was somehow involved.

The houses were spread farther apart now; the older homes were on farm-like tracts of land. Jonathan signaled the boys to stop again. He walked over to an antique mailbox stuck in the dirt near the driveway. *Douglas* was written in an artistic cursive on the side of the box.

Jonathan started to jog down the driveway, motioning the boys to follow. Mark noticed that the modest white house was completely dark in the moonlight. He wondered if the people who lived there were away or if they were in bed already.

The Israelites moved quietly past the house toward the garage at the end of the driveway. Beyond the garage, there was a large garden, where the boys spread out in a circle. Jonathan gave a signal, and the burlap bags were set down. Mark heard a distinct rattling.

Tools? he guessed. *Why do they need tools?*

The bags were opened and flashlights were distributed to everyone. Mark still had no clue what the boys were going to do. He glanced back at the dark house. Were they going to break in?

Everyone moved about with determination, as if they had done this before. Several small garden trowels, weeders and cultivators had been laid out on the burlap bags. Mark shone his flashlight on the garden itself. Part of it was dedicated to flowers, but the majority seemed to contain vegetable plants.

"Weeds," Jonathan whispered in Mark's ear.

"Huh?"

Jonathan directed his flashlight beam to the dirt between the plants. It was filled with thick patches of weeds.

"The weeds are destroying the garden." Jonathan handed Mark a pair of work gloves. "Emma Douglas has been too sick to take care of it. She's also too proud to ask for help, so we're going to do it for her. It'll be a nice gift."

"We came here to weed?" Mark asked with surprise.

"Sure. What did you think we came to do?"

Embarrassed, Mark shrugged.

"All right, gentlemen," Jonathan said in a loud whisper. "Let's get to work. We don't have much time. Whatever you do, be quiet. Don't talk unless you have to, and don't bang your tools around. Attai, I want you and Mark to go to the garage and get the spades, shovels and hoes."

"Won't it be locked?" asked Attai.

"Whit came to visit Emma earlier. He said he made sure it was unlocked for us," explained Jonathan.

Mark was relieved to hear that Whit really was part of this plan.

Attai tugged at Mark's sleeve. "Let's go."

The side door to the garage was unlocked. Mark and Attai had to navigate around Emma's car to reach for the tools they needed. Mark spotted a shovel hanging on the wall next to a small workbench.

"I found a shovel!" Mark said.

"Shh!" Attai returned. "Don't talk."

Attai's tone was unnecessarily harsh, Mark thought. He wondered what he had done to make Attai unfriendly.

Mark saw the spade, rake and hoe hanging near the shovel. He was going to tell Attai but still felt the sting of his last rebuke.

Attai can look around in the wrong places if he wants to, Mark thought, *I'm going to get these tools myself.*

Mark put his flashlight on the workbench and carefully unhooked the shovel from its wall holder. He lowered it by the handle, resting it in the crook of his arm. Then he took down the rake.

From the other side of the garage, Attai saw what Mark had found. "Wait. I'll help you."

"Don't talk," Mark said in a vindictive tone.

"Don't be stupid," Attai replied.

Mark reached up for the hoe, but it was caught on the lip

of the hook. With the rake and shovel still in the crook of his arm, he grabbed the hoe's handle with both hands and shoved upward.

"Don't!" Attai whispered loudly.

Mark was determined to show Attai that he didn't need help, so he pulled down hard on the hoe's handle. This time the hook gave way. The hoe banged against a spade on the wall, making a loud "ching!"

Mark tried to catch the hoe, but as he lurched forward, he stumbled. And all the tools went crashing to the floor.

The sound echoed through the garage and into the quiet night like harsh clanging cymbals. Mark regained his balance and stood still as if the horrifying clatter had frozen him in place.

Attai groaned, ran to the side window and looked out. "They heard you out at the garden," he said. "Let's just hope Emma Douglas was sleeping on her good ear."

Mark, his heart thumping, joined Attai just in time to see a light go on in an upstairs window. Mark gasped with the realization of what he had done.

"Now you did it! You woke her up," Attai said, scrambling toward the open garage door.

Mark remained where he was, still stunned by his own stupidity.

"Come on," Attai called out coarsely. "We have to get out of here!"

CHAPTER SIX

Betrayed

Mark's eyes were still burning when the morning light spread across his room. He lay in his bed remembering every detail of the night before. He felt the same hot humiliation as he recalled the falling tools, the crashing sound and Attai's expression when Emma Douglas's light went on. Scalding embarrassment had washed over him when Jonathan sent them all home. Jonathan had stayed behind to explain to Emma. He didn't want her to be frightened or think she had a prowler.

The last thing Mark remembered seeing was Jonathan standing on the porch, waiting for Emma to answer the door.

Walking home, Attai had lectured Mark about the blunder. "The Israelites are a special group," he said at one point, "and we only accept special people as members."

Mark's mother was still awake and reading in bed when he arrived home. When she asked him how it went, Mark bravely told her everything that had happened, holding back the tears as he explained how he had tried to show off and ruined the mission.

His mother hugged him. "I'm sure they'll still let you join. They wouldn't hold one little mistake against you."

"Yes, they will," Mark argued. "They want members who will move quickly and quietly. They don't want some clumsy oaf."

"I think you're wrong," his mother said gently.

That's what Mark had expected her to say. Mothers didn't really know about things like gangs and how they operate. The decision would rest with Jonathan, Attai and the other Israelites. Mark doubted that even Whit could do anything to help him.

Mark had crawled into bed and stared at the ceiling. He wasn't sure if he had slept, but suddenly it was nine o'clock the next morning, and the phone was ringing in another part of the house.

Moments later, his mother tapped lightly on the door, opened it and peeked in. "Mark?" she said softly.

"Yeah?"

Her tone was hopeful. "That was Whit on the phone. He would like you to come to the shop as soon as you can."

When Mark arrived at Whit's End, the place was already alive with kids moving every which way. Some were browsing in the library. Others were sitting in the restaurant booths talking across the tables. Still other kids were excitedly playing a variety of brightly lit games in the far corner of the house. Mark expected that the county's largest train set, as the banner proclaimed, was in full operation on the second floor. A distant whistle confirmed it.

The sounds merged into a single hum of activity, proclaiming the joy of having fun, of being children. It was a joy that John Avery Whittaker seemed to spread to everyone he met.

But Mark's heart was heavy and refused to be lifted by the spirit of celebration at Whit's End. For the first time, Mark was honestly afraid to see Whit. Mark was sure the Israelites had already told Whit about Mark's goof-up. What would Whit say? How would he break the news that the Israelites had rejected Mark? How would Whit express his own disappointment with Mark?

Mark walked slowly around the counter to where Whit had been working on his ice-cream dispenser the day before. The dispenser was gone, however, and Whit was nowhere to be seen.

Maybe he's in his workroom in the basement, Mark thought.

Rounding the corner to the stairwell that lead down to

the workroom, Mark nearly collided with Whit.

Whit laughed and said, "Fancy running into you here."

"Mom said you wanted me to come."

"I certainly did!" Whit looked around to see if anyone was listening. Then he leaned forward and said quietly, "I heard about what happened last night, and I want you to know that everything has been taken care of. It worked out rather nicely, in fact. A near miracle."

"A miracle?" Mark asked with astonishment.

"When Jonathan explained to Emma Douglas what you boys were up to, she was so touched she said the Israelites could come back any day to finish the job. And if you knew Emma, you would know how much her pride keeps her from asking for help."

Whit smiled and clapped Mark on the shoulder. "See, your little mishap was a blessing in disguise."

Mark frowned. "It doesn't feel like it."

At that moment Mark heard the rumbling of voices in the workroom below. It sounded like an argument.

"I think it's all right to tell you—the Israelites are borrowing my workroom for a meeting," Whit explained. "They're arguing about where to find new secret headquarters."

"New headquarters?"

"Their old tree fort was torn down when the bulldozers cleared the land for a housing development." Whit gestured to the workroom and sighed as the loud voices continued below. "The Israelites do a lot of good things together, but they still argue like a bunch of kids."

Mark tried to figure out what this information should mean to him.

Whit drew Mark closer and said, "What happened to you last night could have happened to anyone. Jonathan knows that. That's why he's the leader."

"But Attai said—"

"Attai can be a bit hotheaded at times. That's why he's not in charge," Whit remarked, pushing Mark along. "Go down to the workroom, and tell them I told you to join the meeting. They haven't voted you in or out yet. It might help if they can talk to you . . . that is, if you still want to be a member."

Mark's face brightened with this new hope. "Are you kidding?"

Whit chuckled. "Go on then."

Mark thanked him and crept down the stairs. The workroom door was closed, but Mark could hear the Israelites clearly. Jonathan was suggesting they build a new tree fort in another part of town. Attai was arguing about doing all that work again.

"There must be a better place to put a secret hideout," he insisted.

When Mark opened the door, all heads turned toward him. He felt himself blush and started to back out again.

"What do you want?" Attai snarled as he leaned forward in his chair, his black eyes blazing.

"Mr. Whittaker told me to come in," Mark said, barely above a whisper.

Attai sat back and replied, "Oh, then I guess our meeting's over."

Jonathan shot Attai a reproving look. "Don't be so rude, Attai."

"What's the point of a meeting about secret headquarters if anybody can come in and listen?" stated Attai. "He's not a member."

"Even more reason for you not to be rude," Jonathan said.

Attai folded his arms defiantly. "Okay, fine. Let's tell the whole world. Maybe Prescott can even suggest a place for us."

Attai turned to Mark and threw the challenge to him. "Can you? I would feel better about you being a member. Maybe you're better at finding hideouts than getting garden tools."

Anger and embarrassment welled up inside Mark. Every instinct in his body wanted to prove Attai wrong. Mark would show him.

"I know a place," Mark began.

All eyes were fixed on him now.

"You do?" Jonathan asked. "A place for us to meet?"

Mark nodded. His heart was pounding. He had to be accepted by the Israelites. At the moment it was all that

mattered.

"It's up by Trickle Lake," he continued. "A hidden cave."

This caused a buzz among the members. Attai's face looked stricken.

"I don't believe you. Where is it?" Attai demanded.

This was what Mark needed. He was in control now. He spoke confidently. "I'll have to show you. Meet me at the Great Tree at two this afternoon."

Mark was in a cold sweat by the time he reached Patti's house. He had to talk to her. He had thought about it the whole walk over; he had to persuade her to join the Israelites. If he could, then maybe—just maybe—she wouldn't be so mad that he had broken his promise to her. Maybe she would understand. He was panic-stricken that she wouldn't.

Mrs. Eldridge greeted him with a smile and showed him to Patti's room. The furniture had been rearranged since he had been there a few days ago. Patti stood in the middle of the room, hands on hips, pondering the walls.

"I think I might paint my room even though I have the other you-know-what to put things in. You want to help me?" she asked without even saying hello.

"I can't right now," Mark muttered. He felt like his thoughts were swimming in his head. What was he going to say to her? How could he talk to her about the cave?

Patti misunderstood his tone. "You're mad at me, aren't

you?"

The question caught Mark off guard.

"You are," she said, "and I don't blame you. I talked to my mom about it, and she said I was being childish. I shouldn't have been so . . . so jealous. I guess that's what it was. If you joined the Israelites, I figured we would never have time to do things together anymore."

Patti sat on her vanity chair and then asked, "Did you meet with them last night?"

"Yeah, I did," said Mark. Maybe he could get her to join the Israelites. If she joined, he could get her to let them use the cave.

"Patti, why don't you join the Israelites with me?" he blurted.

She looked at him curiously.

"They do some really neat things and . . . and we would still have fun together. Just think about it."

"No thanks, Mark."

"Why not?"

"I told you before, I don't want to. I don't care about belonging to a gang. Some of the kids say they're a bunch of snobs, sneaking around, calling each other by those weird names."

Mark pleaded, "It's not like that. They do good things for people. They just keep it a secret, so the people they help won't be embarrassed."

Patti shrugged. "So? I still don't want to join."

"Come on, Patti," Mark said impatiently.

"Mark, you can join if you want. I won't be mad if you do. We can still be friends. Don't worry about me. I'll stop being a baby about it, okay?"

That's not the problem! he wanted to scream, but instead he struggled to think of another approach.

"If you're really my friend, you'll join," he said, knowing it was an unfair thing to say. But he was growing desperate.

Patti winced, as if he had struck her in the face. "What?"

"You heard me."

"I can't believe you could say that. What's wrong with you?"

"Nothing!" he snapped. "I just think you should join. That's all. If you're my friend, you will."

"That's not fair, Mark." Her tone was measured and adultlike. "That's as bad as saying I won't be your friend if you do join."

"Then join!" Mark said, his reasoning getting tangled up in his fear. If she didn't join, he didn't know what he would do. But he could bet his friendship with Patti would be over anyway.

Patti was firm. "I'm not joining, Mark. It's a matter of principle now."

Principles! What do principles have to do with anything? I can't win if she's going to drag principles into it, he thought.

Mark glared at her; then he strode toward the door.

"Where are you going?" she asked.

"I have to go," he snarled in a voice that didn't sound like his own. He stepped into the hall and lingered there for a moment.

Finally, he turned to her again and spoke in a more familiar tone. "Patti, I didn't mean for any of this to happen."

Mark ran down the stairs two at a time and shot out the front door.

He heard Patti call his name, but he didn't stop.

CHAPTER SEVEN

Double Deception

Mark fumed as he walked to Trickle Lake. He was mad at Patti. He was mad at himself. And he was mad at the Israelites. He was mad because his dad had never sent his bike from Washington, D.C., which was why Mark had to walk all the time. He was mad because he had had to move to Odyssey in the first place. The list accumulated with every step toward the Great Tree.

He didn't know why Patti always had to be so stubborn. It would have been easy for her to join the gang. Why couldn't she join? Principles didn't have anything to do with it. She was being selfish. What kind of friend was she anyway? Not much of one to put Mark in this situation.

It's not her cave, he thought. *It's not like she owns a deed to it with her name on it. It doesn't belong to her. Anybody could have found the cave. Who is to say the Israelites didn't find it on their own? Patti doesn't have to know that I showed it to them. She'll just see that it's been taken over by someone else and probably go home and forget about it.*

"Hah! Patti forget about it? Not a chance," Mark muttered aloud to himself.

She would find out who had invaded her secret hiding place. And she would blow a giant fuse when she discovered it was the Israelites.

"Oh, why doesn't she join?" he cried out.

Worse, why had he made the promise not to tell anyone about the cave? He would never make a promise like that to anyone ever again, he decided.

Mark reached the path to Trickle Lake. A hand-carved sign shaped like an arrow said, the Great Tree. The sign also mentioned in small letters that according to legend the person who could climb to the top of the tree could see as far as three counties.

Mark stopped on the path for a moment. *Maybe the Israelites won't show up,* he thought. *Maybe they've found another hideout in the meantime.*

Mark knew it was wishful thinking. They would be there. And he had better have something good to show them.

Maybe he should tell them the truth or part of the truth, he thought. He could explain that he had made a promise to Patti about this secret cave and . . . and . . . he had forgotten he had made the promise. And he could help them come up with another secret hideout. Not a chance. He could see Attai's smug look of satisfaction.

"See," Attai would say, "I told you Prescott didn't deserve to be a member."

Maybe Mark should turn around, go home and not join the gang. Then he could keep his promise to Patti, so they could go on with the summer the way it had been.

But he would lose face with the Israelites for not showing. It was a no-win situation, all because of a stupid cave.

The path took Mark around a short bend that led to The Great Tree. Up ahead the Israelites were sitting by the tree waiting. When one of them pointed at Mark, they all stood.

The Israelites will get more use out of the cave than Patti, Mark assured himself. *All she wants to do is hide her dolls there. The Israelites will do important things, things that could help other people. The Israelites deserve to have that cave. Patti should understand. It's better to upset her than a whole gang.*

"You're late," Jonathan said as Mark approached. "We thought you might not show up."

Mark looked at him coolly. "I had to do a couple of things first."

Attai stepped forward and said, "Well, hotshot, where's this great hiding place of yours?"

This was the moment of truth, Mark realized. He looked at the faces of the Israelites. Were these the faces of his new friends?

"Well?" Attai prodded him.

"Follow me," Mark said.

Mark was silent as he led the gang up the trail. When they reached the spot, he spread aside the green curtain of ivy and stepped into the cave. Everything was exactly as Patti had left it the day before. Mark struck a match and lit the candle wedged in a soda bottle and set it on a crate in the middle of the cave. As the Israelites filed in, their faces registered the same excitement that Mark had felt when he first saw the cave. He knew their imaginations were jumping with the cave's possibilities as a hideout.

"This is an amazing place," said Jonathan.

Attai clapped Mark on the back and exclaimed, "You're all right, Prescott! You may be clumsy with tools, but you know a good hiding place when you see one."

Attai turned to the rest of the Israelites. "What do you think?"

The gang offered their approval through scattered praises: "Great!" "Wow!" "Fantastic!"

"I think we should vote him in," Attai announced.

This was better and faster than Mark could have imagined. What was he so worried about? He was going to become an Israelite.

Jonathan raised his hand. "Hold on, Attai, not so fast. The Israelites don't work that way. We don't vote people out because they make a mistake, and we don't vote people in because they happen to find a good hiding place. You remember the rules. Members are voted in based on their character. Members are seekers of truth. And, above all, they must have a desire to serve people in need."

"We know all that, Jonathan," Attai replied impatiently. "Look, didn't you say in the meeting this morning that Mark would be a good Israelite? Weren't you the one who stuck up for him when I was ready to vote him down?"

Surprised, Mark looked at Jonathan appreciatively.

"Yeah," Jonathan replied, "but I don't want Mark to get the wrong impression. If he is voted in as a member, it must be for the right reason, not because he found a new meeting place for us. Is that understood? Mark was asked to join because of Mr. Whittaker's recommendation."

Again, Mark was surprised.

"Are you saying you don't want to vote?" Attai asked.

Jonathan shook his head. "We can vote. But I would like to ask Mark to leave for a couple of minutes while we do. Do you mind, Mark?"

"Nope," said Mark. They would vote him in, he felt sure. He was going to get what he wanted, the security of new friends, the prestige of a popular gang. Patti would have to understand. Somehow, he would make her understand. This was what he really wanted—Mark, the Israelite.

Suddenly the green curtain was pulled aside. "What's going on in here? What are you doing in my cave?"

Mark gasped and held his breath.

Patti looked around, bewildered, squinting as her eyes adjusted to the darkness. In her arms, she carried a small bag. Everyone remained still. Obviously no one knew how to react to her sudden appearance.

Patti scanned the gawking faces. Then she saw Mark, and her eyes widened.

"You told!" she cried out. The bag slipped from her hands. Dolls and keepsakes tumbled onto the ground. "You promised you wouldn't tell."

Her voice echoed through the cave and into the deepest part of Mark's heart. His mouth moved, but he couldn't force any words out. The eyes of the Israelites fell on him.

Patti started quickly picking up her dolls, stuffing back in the bag as her tears began to fall.

"You told," she said again.

"What's going on?" Jonathan asked, assuming control.

Clutching her bag, Patti stood. "This is my cave. I found it. Mark, you promised." She choked on the words, turned and ran from the cave.

Attai glared at Mark, "What did you promise her?"

Mark swallowed, his throat making a loud clicking

noise. "I promised . . . I . . . I wouldn't tell anyone about this cave."

A collective gasp went through the Israelites.

"Why did you break your promise?" asked Jonathan.

"So you would let me join the Israelites," Mark replied softly.

Mark didn't want to believe this scene was real. He felt a terrible numbness working its way through him.

"I'm sorry you felt you had to do that," Jonathan said. He paused, looking downcast. "As it is, we can't let you become a member, not like this."

Jonathan then turned to Obadiah. "Go tell Patti that her secret is safe with us. It's her cave. We'll find a hideout somewhere else."

The Israelites filed silently out of the cave. Jonathan was the last to leave. He placed his hand gently on Mark's shoulder. "I'm sorry, Mark. You shouldn't have done it. We probably would have voted you in without the cave."

Jonathan stepped through the green curtain; the flow of air caused the candlelight to flicker. Mark remained in the cave alone, thinking until the flame flickered, spat once or twice and went out.

CHAPTER EIGHT

Exiled

I t was the longest week of Mark's life.

After the showdown in the cave, he went home to self-imposed solitary confinement.

It's what I deserve, he thought.

He had lost Patti as a friend by betraying her. The Israelites surely wouldn't have anything to do with him since he was a dishonest promise-breaker. In either case, he couldn't face them. His shame was too great. He would stay home for the rest of the summer. Maybe he could make some new friends when school started. Maybe his mom and dad would get back together really soon, and they would move back to Washington, D.C.

His mother, sensing something was wrong, coaxed the

story out of Mark right after it happened. At first she could only say, "Oh, Mark" over and over again.

That didn't make him feel any better.

Then she tried to explain that she understood how he must feel. "It's a lot like what happened to your father and me. We hurt each other. Now, we're paying for it in this time apart, in the slow, painful process of repairing our trust."

Again, Mark wasn't encouraged. He wanted to be able to go to Patti, apologize and make everything the way it was before.

He knew better. It was a lesson he had already learned once. Things don't change back to the way they were before. Somehow, he had to deal with the way things were now. But how?

Mark wrote a letter to Patti, tore it up, started over, tore that one up. He started again and then gave up. He also tried to write a letter to the Israelites addressed to Jonathan, but he couldn't do that either.

He wanted to explain to them all. He wanted them to understand why he had done it. But the explanation didn't read right. Once he wrote, "I'm sorry," everything else seemed meaningless. And only the words "I'm sorry" on the page didn't seem like enough.

Mark had to pay some sort of penance. Punishment, that's what he needed, so he hid at home.

"This is a coward's way out," his mother said. "If you

face up to what you did and apologize, I'm sure things will get better. You don't have to lock yourself in the house."

Mark simply nodded and returned to the book he was reading or the television show he was trying to watch or the letter he was trying to write to his father.

His mother couldn't even persuade him to go to town with her to run errands.

Whit's End was off-limits as far as he was concerned. He kept picturing himself entering the shop and facing a silent, staring crowd. "He's the one," they would say. "He double-crossed his best friend and tricked the Israelites." "Stay away from him." "He's trouble."

Then Whit would ask him to leave. "Sorry, Mark, we can't have kids like you in here."

More than once, Mark looked away from his book or the TV with tears in his eyes. Eventually his guilt gave way to a highly dramatic self-pity. He would be a loner from now on. A stranger to everyone. A boy without a name. Isolated and friendless, he would become nothing more than a shadow on the wall. Those feelings lasted for a day.

Later in the week, the isolation turned into boredom, and the boredom led to a quiet ache deep inside him. He didn't really care about the Israelites anymore. It would have been neat to be part of their gang. They were fun and exciting, but it didn't matter as much as it had before—not as much as Patti mattered. He missed her.

He lost count of the times he would be reading a book and wanted to tell Patti about the good parts. He remembered their walks in the woods when she introduced him to all the secret places of Odyssey. He thought about how they had met, how he had mistaken her for a bully and pulled her off Joe Devlin just as she was about to win the fight. Later, she had helped Mark solve the mystery of who had slashed the tire on Joe's new bike.

Mark couldn't remember when he decided to be friends with Patti. He probably never really decided at all. It happened the way friendships are meant to happen. They stopped trying to impress each other. They didn't need to pretend they were tough or cool or brave. They could tell each other things they wouldn't dare breathe to anyone else. They simply became friends.

Now the thought of losing Patti's friendship nagged at him. He didn't want to be an outcast or a loner or feel sorry for himself for the rest of his life. He wanted to make up with her. Somehow, he had to make her trust him again. It was a matter of principle. If only he could talk to her . . .

It was nearly dinnertime when Mark replaced the receiver on its cradle again; the phone was still busy. Someone at her house had been on the phone for a long time. His stomach tightened, wondering if Patti had taken the phone off the hook to keep from talking to him. It had been a week; would she do something like that after such a long time? He sat back on his mother's bed to consider

the answer. It didn't matter, he decided. If she wouldn't talk on the phone, he would go to her house.

He had just stepped into the upstairs hallway when he heard someone knock at the front door.

He waited at the top of the stairs, listening to his mom walk to the door, open it and then exclaim, "What a surprise! Come on in."

A deep, resonant voice responded with appreciation.

Whit! What's he doing here? Mark questioned.

He didn't move. His mind rifled through all the reasons Whit would come to his house.

"Is Mark home?" Whit asked.

"Yes, he's here. I'll go get him," replied his mother.

The bannister rattled, and the steps creaked as his mother started up the stairs. She stopped halfway and called, "Mark? You have a visitor."

Mark's heart picked up its pace. *Is Whit going to talk to me about the Israelites? Will he lecture me for betraying Patti?*

Mark felt like he was walking in shoes filled with heavy stones as he went down the steps into the living room. Whit and his mom both turned with expressions of concern when Mark entered. His fear about what Whit might say increased.

"Hello, Mark," Whit said, extending his hand.

Mark took it, and they shook hands awkwardly.

"Hi, Mr. Whittaker."

"I haven't seen you around in a while. Whit's End isn't the same without you," Whit said with a smile.

"I . . . I've been busy."

Doesn't he know? Mark wondered. *Didn't anyone tell him what happened?*

"I stopped by to see if you've talked to Patti today."

"Patti? No, I haven't talked to her in . . . well . . . a week."

Whit raised an eyebrow curiously and then went on. "Oh, that's a shame. Then you haven't heard anything about her."

This line of questioning worried Mark. "No, why? Is something wrong?"

"We hope not," Whit replied. "Patti left early this morning. She was supposed to be home for lunch and a one o'clock dentist appointment, but she didn't show up. She's still missing."

"Patti's missing?" Mark asked with surprise.

Whit nodded gravely. "Her parents said it's not like her. They've been checking all the usual places, calling everyone they thought might know something. I think they tried here, but the line was busy."

"I haven't been on the phone," his mother said. "Mark?"

Mark thought of Patti's parents trying to call him while he was trying to call Patti.

"I was on the phone," he replied.

Whit continued, "The police are now looking for her.

Some volunteers have joined the search, too."

The image of all those people searching for Patti made Mark realize how serious it was. What if something bad happened to her? Where could she be?

"Has anyone tried around Trickle Lake?" Mark asked.

"I'm sure they have," answered Whit. "Why? Do you know something we don't?"

For a moment Mark considered his promise to Patti. Just because he blabbed to the Israelites didn't mean he should blab to anyone else. But what if something had happened to Patti in the cave? It wouldn't be wrong to break his promise, would it?

Whit looked straight into Mark's eyes and said, "If you know something, Mark, it's important that you tell me. Anything could help."

CHAPTER NINE

The Search

Bouncing along in Whit's car to Trickle Lake, Mark told Whit about the cave and the painful story related to it.

Whit's face lit up with renewed understanding. "That explains a few things. You see, the Israelites didn't tell me why they voted you down for the group. And Patti hasn't been to Whit's End all week. I assumed she was with you."

Mark was surprised that everyone had kept quiet about what he had done to her.

"It must have been a miserable week for both of you," Whit observed.

"I'll bet she's glad to get rid of me," Mark replied dejectedly. "I don't know if she'll ever want to be friends again."

Whit glanced at Mark sympathetically. "I don't believe that for a minute. The ties that make up a good friendship are stronger than a single wrong."

"But I betrayed her," Mark cried helplessly.

"Yes, well, that will take some time to fix. But your friendship can be mended, Mark, if you're willing to work at it."

"I am! But I don't know if she'll want to."

Whit reached across the front seat and touched Mark's arm. "First let's find her; then we'll see."

Mark gazed ahead as they approached the sparkling mountain lake and parked the car.

"There's a large flashlight under your seat. I think we'll need it," Whit said.

At the lake, the usual quiet was broken by a handful of volunteers who had spread into the surrounding hills and mountains to look for Patti.

"There are so many people," Mark observed.

"It's one of the advantages of living in a small town," Whit noted. "They don't waste any time when it comes to lost children."

Mark and Whit walked to a small dock on the north side of the lake, where a police officer was standing near his car.

The officer greeted Whit warmly and shook Mark's hand when they were introduced. Though he spoke directly to both of them, he kept glancing out at two powerboats moving in slow circles around the lake.

The officer's brow was furrowed into deep crevices. "I hate it when things like this come up. I have a daughter of my own, you know."

"Mark is going to lead me to a place where Patti liked to play," Whit explained.

"Holler if you find anything," the officer replied.

"Of course we will."

The officer looked back at the lake and sighed, "It's a sad business."

Mark watched the powerboats move through another cycle. Then he noticed people leaning over the sides of each boat, staring into the water. He trembled as he realized they were looking for Patti beneath the lake's gentle ripples.

Alarmed, Mark tugged at Whit's sleeve.

Whit nodded, said goodbye to the officer and walked quickly to the path leading to The Great Tree.

"Do they really think Patti's drowned?" Mark asked with a quivering voice.

"They have to consider everything," Whit said matter-of-factly. "Patti's parents knew she often came up here."

"She's in the cave," Mark declared, willing it to be true.

They walked in silence, their breathing providing a natural rhythm to their steps. Mark motioned for Whit to follow him and took the lead as they navigated their way around the dense brush and trees.

"Here we are," Mark said when they were only a short way from the green curtain.

Whit glanced around. Spotting the camouflaged hillside, he remarked, "Ah, it's through there I'll wager."

"How did you know that?" Mark asked with astonishment.

Whit smiled as he moved toward the hill. "I used to be a Boy Scout."

They spread aside the green curtain and stepped into the cave. It was coal black. Turning on his flashlight, Whit went farther in, shifting the beam from object to object. Mark was jolted by the shining faces and sparkling eyes that peered back at them.

Patti's dolls, he thought sadly.

She had obviously done some redecorating since Mark had been there a week ago. Not only were the crates still there, but she had also added small boxes that served as seats for the dolls. She had laid thick branches across evenly matched stones as shelves for knickknacks and trinkets.

"A home away from home," Whit said.

"Patti," Mark called. His voice sounded hollow and empty.

They stood still and waited.

"Patti, are you here?" Whit shouted.

No answer.

Mark's heart sank. He thought for sure she would be there. Where else could she be?

"I guess I was wrong," he said.

"This is such a well-formed cave. I wonder if . . ." Whit mused aloud, shining the light to the rear of the cave. "Hmm, an unfinished mine shaft?"

"It seems to go farther back, but Patti and I didn't go there," Mark said, failing to mention that they had been afraid.

Stooping to accommodate the incline of the ceiling, Whit followed the beam deeper into the darkness. Mark stayed close behind. They crept along for a short distance. The air was becoming noticeably thick with an earthy damp odor. They stopped before a wall of rock.

"It looks like a dead end," Whit observed. "Rock and shadow make it look deeper than it is."

Again, Mark was disappointed. "We figured it went back for miles."

"A lot of the caves around here do, but not this one." Whit turned to Mark and said, "Let's get out of here."

Something about the movement of the flashlight beam on the cave wall caught Mark's eye. It bent into a peculiar shadow, he thought. Maybe it was a trick of the darkness. Whit didn't seem to notice.

"Watch your head," Whit advised as he started to leave.

Mark lingered a moment, and then said, "Whit?"

"Yeah, Mark?"

"I think there's something back here," he said timidly. If the shadow had been an optical illusion, he would feel embarrassed.

"What is it?" questioned Whit.

"I'm not sure." Mark pointed off to the side of the dead end. "Over there. It's a weird shadow."

Whit focused the beam on an area about ten feet away. "That's not a shadow!" Whit said, his breath quickening. "The cave bends around to the right!"

"No wonder we didn't see it," added Mark.

"An old miner's trick," Whit explained as they inched along. "Miners used to dig the entryway to the shafts at such an angle; then unwanted visitors would think there were no shafts at all."

Whit and Mark passed from the cave into a bigger area braced with large timber beams. The air thickened, and Mark found himself breathing harder.

"We have to be very careful," cautioned Whit. "Whoever dug this mine didn't do a very good job. To tell the truth, I'm not sure we're very smart to be in here."

Mark was about to protest when his foot struck something. It made a banging sound like he had hit metal. Mark jumped back, hitting his back against the wall.

"Ouch!" he cried out.

"What's this? A well-preserved lantern?" Whit asked as he bent to look at it. Then he answered his own question. "Nope, it's new. There's a price tag on it from

McIntyre's Hardware in town."

"It's Patti's! She's got to be in here somewhere," Mark exclaimed, picking up the lantern. The glass surrounding the wick was shattered.

Mark stepped forward to continue his search.

"Mark!" Whit cried out, jerking the boy back.

"What's wrong?" Mark asked with alarm.

"Look!" Whit pointed the flashlight to the ground in front of Mark. It continued ahead for three steps and then disappeared into a black hole.

"It's a deep shaft. Are you trying to break your neck?" asked Whit.

Mark gasped, fell to his knees beside the hole and called out, "Patti!"

Whit knelt next to Mark and guided the light into the hole. A wooden ladder with broken rungs was hanging loosely until it almost touched the black gravel at the bottom.

"Twenty feet deep, I figure," Whit said.

Then Mark saw the sneaker on the bottom like a strange white spot in an inkwell.

"There!" he shouted.

Whit adjusted the flashlight, so it would flood the area with a brighter beam of light. On the floor the small figure of a girl lay like a randomly tossed doll. It was Patti.

CHAPTER TEN

The Scene Played Out

Mark sat in the hospital waiting room, battling the thick weariness that had threatened to take over his mind and body ever since he and Whit had found Patti. The numbness was winning. In a dream-like haze, Mark recalled everything that had happened.

Whit had sent him for help. Mark had run from the cave through the woods screaming as loudly as his aching lungs would let him. The police had come quickly. Then the paramedics. Under generator-powered lights, they had strapped Patti onto a stretcher and brought her out. Her parents, notified that she had been found, had stood nearby, watching anxiously. She was alive, everyone was assured, but no one knew how badly she had been hurt.

Mark's mother appeared eventually; he didn't know when. Together, they drove to the hospital in nearby Connellsville, where Patti had been taken. Now Mark waited with his mother, Whit and the Eldridges's for word from the doctor.

Down the hall, someone laughed. *Nobody should laugh in a place like this, at a time like this,* Mark thought.

He didn't know much about hospitals, but he had seen movies and the laughter just didn't seem right.

What if Patti's so broken they can't fix her? he wondered. *What if she has to be in a wheelchair for the rest of her life? What if she isn't herself ever again? She could forget who she is. Would I, could I, still be her friend?*

"There could be brain damage after a fall like that," someone had whispered.

Mark squeezed his eyes shut, trying to block out the terrible thoughts. A tear slipped down his cheek.

What if she dies? What if the damage is worse than everyone thought it would be, and the doctor comes and says, "I'm sorry; we did all we could"?

Did people die from falls like that? Of course they did. Patti could die. Mark felt as if his mind were screaming with such awful possibilities.

Then he would never be able to apologize to Patti. This past miserable week would stretch out into forever. And he would never have another friend like her.

"Oh, God," Mark prayed silently, "don't let anything

bad happen to Patti. Don't let her die. Please."

He felt someone touch his hand and opened his eyes.

"Mark, are you all right?" his mother asked softly.

Mark's eyelashes were thick with tears. He had been crying and hadn't even realized it.

"Yeah," he sniffled.

Whit knelt in front of Mark and looked at him intently. "Mark, I hope you understand that no matter what happens with Patti, you're a good friend to her. We don't know how long she would have lasted if you hadn't known about the cave."

Mark couldn't accept a word of it. How could he? He had betrayed her.

"You broke a promise," Whit said, as if reading Mark's mind. "But all of us hurt others at one time or another, especially those we care about the most. That's the risk of loving. We allow ourselves to get close enough to be hurt. Do you understand?"

Mark nodded, though he still wasn't sure he could be comforted.

Whit continued, "Friendship can seem fragile. But the love that creates friendship is made up of pretty tough stuff. That's the kind of love God gives us. And with that love, He gives the ability to forgive. I'm certain Patti cares for you and forgives you no matter how terrible you think you've been to her. Believe me."

Just as Whit stood, a doctor with a stethoscope draped

around her neck walked into the waiting room and gestured to Patti's parents. They followed her to the opposite
side of the hallway. The doctor spoke in a low whisper.
She used her hands while she talked, as if referring to an
invisible diagram. Shortly, Mrs. Eldridge began to cry and
held her husband's arm tighter. Mark's mother, also
watching the three of them, tensed and drew Mark closer.

This is how it happens in the movies, Mark thought.
This is how they break the terrible news.

He prepared himself for the worst. He wondered if people would feel sorry for him, the best friend of the girl who
had died so young.

Ex-best friend, he reminded himself. And it stung.

The doctor moved off down the hallway, and Patti's
parents returned to the waiting room. Mark sat up and
braced himself for the news.

Mr. Eldridge, struggling with the words, his voice
catching, finally said, "She'll be all right. She suffered a
slight concussion, bruised some ribs and broke her right
arm. But . . . all things considered, she'll be all right."

"We're so thankful," Mrs. Eldridge choked through her
tears.

It was another day before Mark was allowed to see Patti
at the hospital. It had been a long day to end a very long
week. He rehearsed what he would say to her, imagining
the scene over and over again in his mind. He checked and
double-checked every word he would say. He had to say it

perfectly with the right tone. Mark was desperate for Patti to know how sorry he was.

His mother waited in the hall while Mark went into the room first. Mrs. Eldridge opened the door and gestured for Mark to enter. Then she closed the door and joined Mark's mother in the hall.

Mark passed an empty hospital bed, the sheets starched stiff and white. He couldn't imagine anyone sleeping in such a hard bed. He peered around a curtain suspended from the ceiling by movable hooks. Patti was sitting on her bed, which was covered with get-well cards and gifts. Patti looked like Patti, Mark was relieved to see. Except, she had a small bandage on her forehead and a milk-white cast on her right arm that went up to her elbow.

"Hi, Patti," Mark said.

"Oh," she remarked, glancing at him with no special recognition, "hi."

He moved closer to the bed. "You have a cast," he observed.

She nodded. "It itches."

"Are you going to get everyone to sign it?"

She frowned. "No, my dad said he would draw a picture on it. Maybe ducks flying south for the winter."

"Ducks! On a cast? Nobody draws ducks on a cast. You want something cool," Mark contended.

"I'll have ducks if I want to. Don't tell me what to put on my cast."

"All right, all right. Have ducks."

This isn't how the scene is supposed to be played out, Mark thought.

Seconds passed as they both looked around the room awkwardly. Then Patti broke the silence. "Mom and Dad said you found me in that hole."

"Yeah."

"I guess I ought to thank you," she said without a hint of gratitude.

"Forget about it."

"Thanks, anyway." She let out a sigh and then said, "There. I wanted to be able to tell my parents I thanked you. You'll tell them, right? If they ask."

"Yeah, sure," he said. "How did you wind up in that shaft anyway?"

Patti shrugged. "I was unpacking some of my stuff, and a ball fell out of the bag. I thought it bounced to the back of the cave, so I went after it. Then I found that other cave. I got curious. I thought maybe I would find buried treasure. Pretty dumb."

"I would have done the same thing," Mark offered.

"Like I said, pretty dumb," she countered. "I dropped my lantern when I fell. I don't remember anything after that."

"Did you get your ball back?"

"No."

Mark brightened. "Maybe I can find it for you."

"You don't have to do that."

"I can if I want," he said.

Why is she being so difficult? he wondered.

"Don't do me any favors," Patti replied. "I want to get my dolls and stuff out of the cave anyway."

"You do?"

"Yeah. What good is a secret cave when everybody knows about it? Tell your Israelite friends they can have it if they want it."

Okay, Mark thought, *she's still mad.*

"They're not my Israelite friends anymore."

"They aren't?" Patti asked with disbelief. "Why not?"

He shrugged. "Because I broke my promise to you. Didn't they tell you?"

"No," she said and then nodded. "It makes sense, though."

Mark just wanted to get out of there. He hesitated and looked out the window at nothing in particular. Now that he was finally in a position to apologize to her, he wasn't sure he could do it.

Yes, he had broken his promise, but did she really have the right to be mad after a whole week? After all, he was the one who had suffered sitting home alone, watching dumb TV programs. And what did she do? She decorated her cave like nothing had happened. It hadn't affected her one bit. He hadn't even gotten to be an Israelite either! The least she could do was be a little nicer when he was leading up to an apology.

He flinched. What was he thinking? Was he losing his mind? He took a deep breath.

"Patti," he began exactly as he had rehearsed it at home.

"What?" Her tone was hard, as if she expected a fight.

He paused and glared at her. "I've been practicing all day, and this isn't working the way it's supposed to. You're making it really hard."

"What are you talking about?"

"This whole conversation," Mark complained. "I was supposed to tell you as soon as I came in."

"Tell me what?"

"Tell you that I'm sorry for breaking my promise to you. I . . . I betrayed you, and I've been miserable all week about it. I won't blame you if you don't want to be my friend anymore, but I'm . . . I'm still very, very sorry. Okay? I just wanted you to know that. I hope you can . . . you know . . . forgive me."

He considered making an escape right then, but he couldn't get his feet to move.

Patti shrugged indifferently. "I guess I can," she said.

"Huh?"

"Forgive you."

"You can?" Mark asked.

"Yeah, but . . ."

"What?"

"It still makes me mad when I think about it."

"That's okay."

"And it might make me mad for a little while after this," she added.

"That's okay, too," Mark said, glad to make any concession. "You can be mad and still be my friend at the same time, can't you?"

"Yeah, I guess I can. Mom and Dad do it all the time." She looked at Mark thoughtfully. "But it'll take a while. I mean, before we can be friends like we were. It'll be a long time before I can tell you any secrets again."

Mark relaxed. "Yeah, I figured. This kind of thing always takes time. I've been watching my parents."

Another lapse in conversation followed, but it was less awkward. Mark felt a peculiar sense of peace within. The room seemed brighter and warmer.

He considered what she had just said and asked, "What kind of secrets can't you tell me?"

Patti thought about it for a moment. "Any kind," she replied.

"You have some right now?"

"I might."

"Like what?" asked Mark.

"I can't tell you. That's why they're secrets."

"Come on," Mark said, coaxing her.

"No!"..

"I won't tell anyone this time," he promised.

"Mark!" she glared angrily.

But Mark thought he saw a hint of a smile.

CHAPTER ELEVEN

A Pleasant Surprise

I t was a couple more days before Patti was allowed to go home. Mark had spent that time working feverishly. He wanted to prove he could be her friend again.

Exhausted, he stood on the Eldridges's front porch waiting for Patti's parents to bring her home that afternoon. When they pulled into the driveway, they lingered at the car, gathering her things from the backseat and trunk. As Patti mounted the steps to the porch, she still looked like the survivor of a battle. A smaller bandage now adorned her forehead; her cast was neatly cradled in a sling.

"Hi, Mark," Patti said. "What are you doing here?"

"I was in the neighborhood and thought I'd stop by," he replied.

"Oh, I guess you can come on in."

"If Mr. Prescott would be so kind," Mr. Eldridge said, as he dropped Patti's suitcase at Mark's feet.

"Patti, why don't you show Mark where you want this in your room?" suggested Mr. Eldridge.

"Lead on, Maid Marian," Mark said, gesturing grandly as he picked up the suitcase.

Patti shot him an uncomfortable glance. She wasn't ready to be Maid Marian yet, Mark concluded.

As she stepped into the house, she wrinkled her nose and sniffed the air. "Dad must be working on something in the garage again."

Mark didn't answer but followed her quietly down the hall and up the stairs. When they rounded the bannister into the hallway, Patti's bedroom door was closed.

"Why did they close it?" she asked with a frown. Suddenly she turned on Mark. "All right, what's going on?"

"We all have our secrets, Patti," Mark answered with a smile.

"If this is some kind of trick, Mark Prescott," she threatened, "just remember, you're not on anybody's best-seller list this week."

"Hurry up, Patti, this suitcase is heavy. Will you just open the door, please?"

She growled, threw open the door and gasped.

Her room was painted in a rich tone of forest green. The bedspread, canopy and curtains were a complimentary shade. At the foot of the bed, her dolls and keepsakes and everything she had taken to the cave were spread out in a carefully arranged display around three crates and the lantern with the broken glass. A copy of a book about Robin Hood and another one about pirates were propped up on two of the crates.

Patti exclaimed, "You? You did all this?"

Mark felt himself blushing. "Your parents helped."

"Mark!" she cried, tears forming in her eyes.

"Does that mean you like it?" he asked, hesitating. "I mean, it's not the cave."

Patti looked at him silently for several seconds, enough to make Mark squirm. He knew she liked it, but he wasn't sure what she was going to do. He tensed, thinking she might try to kiss him or something crazy like that. He didn't want her to get mushy. He just wanted her to be his friend again.

She smiled. Maybe she understood what he was feeling because she didn't do anything to him or say another word. She simply walked into her room and looked it over proudly.

Other books by Paul McCusker

Youth Ministry Comedy & Drama: Better Than Bathrobes but Not Quite Broadway
(co-author Chuck Bolte; Group Books)

Plays

Snapshots & Portraits
(Lillenas Publishing Co.)
Camp W
(Contemporary Drama Service)
Family Outings
(Lillenas Publishing Co.)
The Revised Standard Version of Jack Hill
(Baker's Play Publishing Co.)
Catacombs
(Lillenas Publishing Co.)
The Case of the Frozen Saints
(Baker's Play Publishing Co.)
The Waiting Room
(Baker's Play Publishing Co.)
A Family Christmas
(Contemporary Drama Service)
The First Church of Pete's Garage
(Baker's Play Publishing Co.)
Home for Christmas
(Baker's Play Publishing Co.)

Sketch Collections

Void Where Prohibited
(Baker's Play Publishing Co.)
Some Assembly Required
(Contemporary Drama Service)
Quick Skits & Discussion Starters
(co-author Chuck Bolte; Group Books)
Vantage Points
(Lillenas Publishing Co.)
Batteries Not Included
(Baker's Play Publishing Co.)
Souvenirs
(Baker's Play Publishing Co.)
Sketches of Harvest
(Baker's Play Publishing Co.)

Musicals

The Meaning of Life & Other Vanities
(co-author Tim Albritton; Baker's Play Publishing Co.)